THE FOG'S NET

PAT PFLIEGER   *Illustrated by* RUTH GAMPER

Houghton Mifflin Company

Boston 1994

For Uel, who loved picture books—P. P.

For Benjamin and Adam—R. G.

Text copyright © 1994 by Pat Pflieger
Illustrations copyright © 1994 by Ruth Gamper

Library of Congress Cataloging-in-Publication Data

Pflieger, Pat.
The fog's net / by Pat Pflieger ; illustrated by Ruth Gamper.
p.   cm.
Summary: Devora agrees to weave a net for the fog in order to keep
her brother safe, but when the fog breaks its word, she has to find
another way to save him.
ISBN 0-395-68194-4
[1. Fog—Fiction.   2. Weaving—Fiction.   3. Brothers and sisters—
Fiction.]   I. Gamper, Ruth, ill.   II. Title.
PZ7.P448559Fo   1994   93-31512
[E]—dc20   CIP
                              AC

Printed in the United States of America

HOR   10   9   8   7   6   5   4   3   2   1

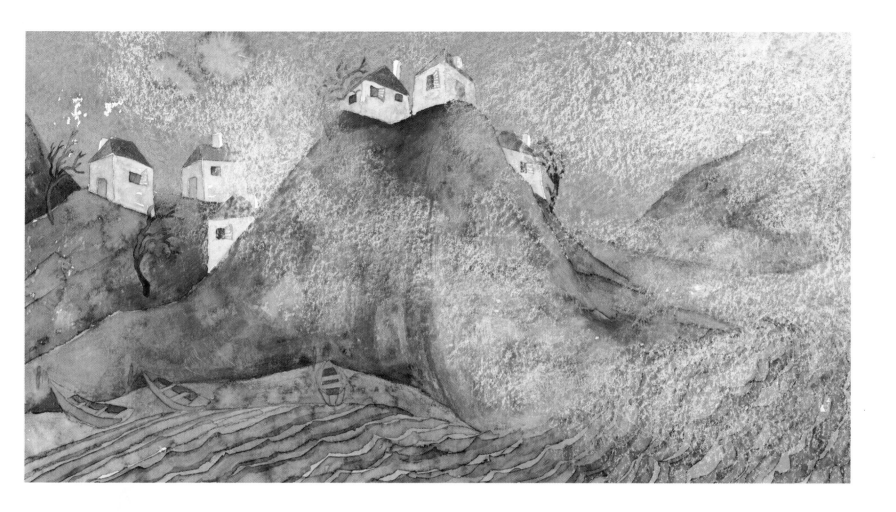

Once there was a village by the sea where, when the fog drifted in, thick and cold and grey, boats and people would disappear. "The mist is hungry," the villagers would say. "It has cast its nets for food."

Devora the weaver knew the truth of it, for one morning, walking by the cold, dark sea, she found a torn piece of net. It was strong and tightly knotted, but it was grey and cold and wet, and it slid through her fingers as if it were a cloud.

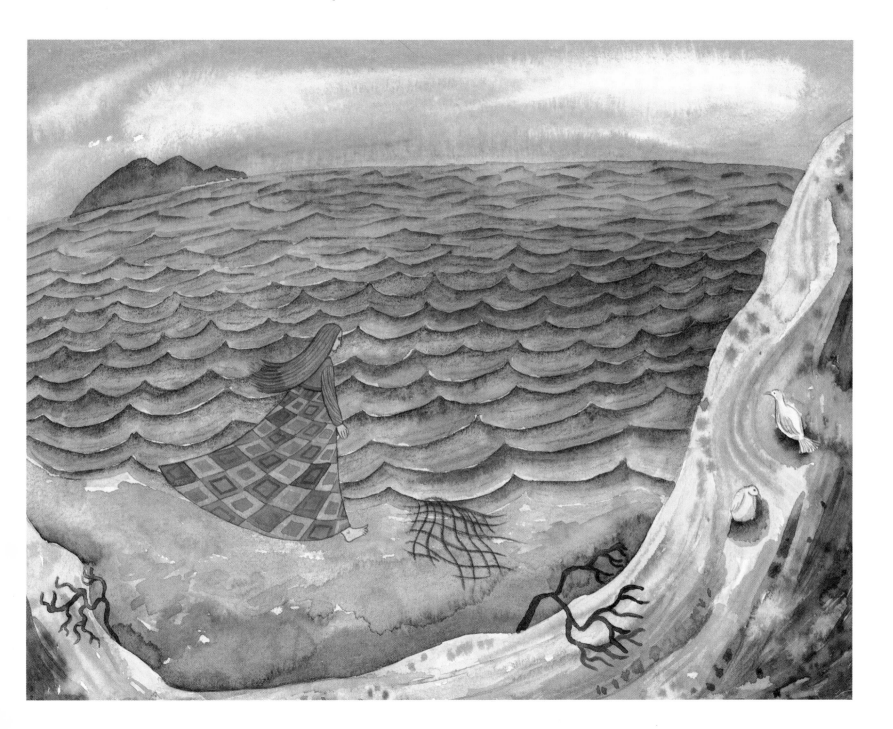

Devora lived in a cottage on the cliffs with her brother Jarem and their baby sister Christaba. They lived alone, for their parents had gone fishing one day and vanished in the fog. Jarem caught fish and dug clams and picked fat berries for them to eat. Sometimes he worked on the little boats of fishermen. Christaba laughed at Jarem's funny faces and played with the brass bell that swung from the hood of her cradle. Devora spun fine yarn and wove it into coverlets and cloaks and yards of soft cloth. And, like her mother before her, she made nets for the fishermen.

Late one night she was weaving a bride's coverlet and singing softly to herself when there was a rattle of the latch and a whisper at the door. When Devora opened it, she found nothing outside but the night and the fog.

"Who is it?" she called softly.

There was stillness and then a whisper: "Devora! I need a net woven."

Devora thought she knew who it was, but still she said, "Come in and sit by the fire where it is warm."

"No, Devora," said the whisper from the fog. "Weave for me, weaver. I would that my net were larger and stronger. Weave for me. I have brought you the twine." And sure enough, a bobbin of twine lay at the doorstep—thick and grey.

Devora thought for a moment, for she knew it was the fog she talked to, not some fisherman.

"Fog," she said, "I'll not weave for you."

And the fog answered, "Then I will weave. I will weave a shroud of mist for you and yours to wander in. You will lose your Jarem in it, and if I cannot have my net, at least I will have your brother."

Devora's heart wept at the thought of those who would lose family if she made the net, but she had no choice, for she'd lose Jarem if she did not.

"And if I weave, what shall my payment be?" she asked the fog.

"I'll not touch you, nor yours, nor any that you favor," said the fog.

And so Devora made the bargain.

That night she hardly rested, for she was thinking and planning. The next day she began to weave with the thick twine the fog had given her. Awful stuff it was to work with, for it was cold and slippery as a cloud. But bit by bit Devora made a net that hung grey and wet, light as the mist but strong. She took no joy in its making, and neither did Christaba, for Devora took the bell from her cradle to tie into a corner.

The night the net was finished, Devora stepped outside the cottage and found the fog waiting for her, an end of its net crumpled on the doorstep. With sure fingers Devora attached the new section to the old.

"You have done well, Devora!" said the fog. "You and yours are safe."

But Devora went back into the cottage with a sad heart, for she knew that others would be caught in the fog's great net.

And caught they were, for the very next day the mist crept in, and that evening Jarem did not come home. Devora had sent him out with some fishermen, hoping that if the fog would not touch any she loved, then it would not touch those Jarem was with. But now she stood on the cliff and wept, for the fog had not kept its bargain.

She bundled Christaba close and warm and snuggled her into a basket. Christaba's laugh was the only bright thing in the fog as Devora carried her down to the beach to Jarem's little boat.

Onto the water in the tiny boat she went, with Christaba chattering while Devora rowed out, out, out onto the sea.

The fog swallowed them. It was like rowing through a cloud. She could not tell where they were going, but she rowed and she rowed, and she listened and she listened, until she heard a tiny golden sound, the sound of a brass bell bobbing on the water—Christaba's bell jingled by the waves.

She rowed and she rowed until she found the little bell tied to the corner of the net she had made. She untied the bell and returned it to Christaba. The net she hooked to the boat so it trailed behind as she rowed, finding her way back toward shore.

The rowing out was long, but the rowing home seemed longer. The net itself was not heavy as it trailed behind the boat, but what it held was heavy as stones.

At last she heard the shush of the waves on the beach and knew she was home. She landed the boat and hauled it onto the shore. Devora was weary from rowing, but her task was not yet done. On the beach she built a fire of driftwood and whatever she could find to burn. She built the fire as high and as hot as she could, for what she needed to burn was wet.

Devora unhooked the net from the boat and began to pull and walk with it, dragging it up the beach. The net was heavy, and it stretched out and vanished into the foggy sea. But desperation made her strong. Bit by bit the net came onto the beach. Devora dragged the corner to the fire and put it there to burn. Then she walked down to the water's edge to haul in another section of the great net that dripped water and seaweed. Another section to burn; then down to the water for more. It was exhausting. She was afraid she could not finish.

Then from the sea came shouting—fishermen calling to the shore. Devora heard Jarem's voice, and her heart grew light. And from the sea came splashing —fishermen swimming to the shore. And there was Jarem, wet as a seal, hugging her tight.

The joyful fishermen took the net from Devora. They knew their work, and they set up a chant to work by as they hauled in the fog's grey net. Other things came with it: bits of wood to feed to the fire; exhausted birds to warm and release; their own small boats; other boats of strangers, terribly empty. People from the village came to see what was burning. Gladly they joined the fishermen hauling in the net. They gathered more wood to keep the fire high and hot, for the fog's damp net was hard to burn.

The net was darker now: an older section, black with age. Still they hauled and burned. The smoke from the net mingled with the fog. Still they hauled and burned. The net was even darker: an even older section. But the fog seemed lighter now, as if the moon were breaking through.

From the fog there came a terrible wail: "My net! My beautiful net! What are you doing to my beautiful net?" Only Devora heard it, for the others were chanting too loudly. She cradled Christaba and shivered.

They hauled and burned, hauled and burned. The sky grew lighter and lighter. The net they burned was as black as the bottom of the sea. "My net!" The fog's wail had fallen to a whisper. "What are you doing to my beautiful net?"

They hauled and burned, hauled and burned. Now something pale came in, flailing and gasping. A cry arose, for it was a stranger, a fisherman from the lands to the north. He crawled onto the shore, and he knelt there, coughing. He was gathered up and taken to the fire to be warmed.

Then the net grew narrower, and the net grew lighter; and then they had hauled in all of it and were burning the last section. The fog had faded and the moon shone on the rippling sea. The stars danced bright. "My net!" Devora heard, fading in the night sky.

The fishermen and the village folk stood around the fire, watching the last of the net burn and looking at the stranger. He stood in damp clothes that steamed from the heat, and he looked back at them.

"You and yours have rescued me," he said. "And I thank you for it."

"It was Devora," someone answered, and the stranger looked at her.

"I thank you, Devora," he said. "I thought not to be rescued at all. There is a land where the fog goes, out beyond the sight of our homes. Bright and warm the land is when the fog is off hunting, but cold and dark when the fog is at home. There I've lived with others captured by the fog. We weep for our homes and for those we have left on these far shores. Today, when I saw that the net was being pulled this way, I took my heart in my hands and leapt into the net, with a piece of wood to carry me. I hoped it would take me home.

"Now that the net is gone, I can guide you back. We can sail there and bring the others home to those they weep for."

Around the fire shouts were raised, and around the fire plans were made. Devora cradled Christaba and laughed to think of their parents coming home. She looked often at the handsome stranger standing in the firelight, and he looked back at her.

The next day the villagers sailed with the stranger to the island beyond all sight of home and fetched back those they had lost to the fog. Now Devora and Jarem and Christaba lived happily with their parents in the cottage by the sea. Soon Devora was weaving coverlets for her wedding to the fisherman from the north.

Strangely enough, the fog stayed away from the village. Oh, sometimes there was a bit of mist, a wisp that the sun soon melted; but the fog thick as a cloud did not return, and all that remained of it was a story that people told around the fire on cold winter nights.

Little Chico

Mama Jumbo

Juju

Buti

For Jude—Love, N.D.

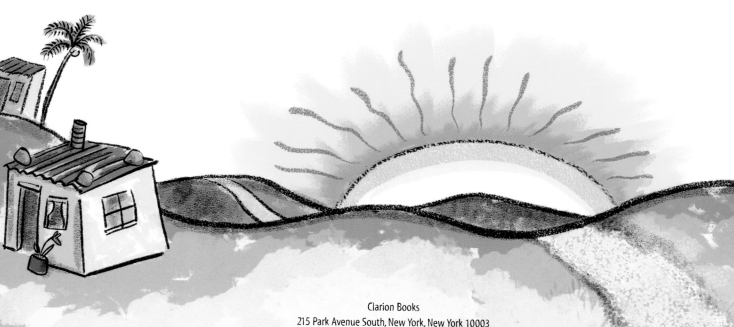

Clarion Books
215 Park Avenue South, New York, New York 10003
Copyright © 2012 by Niki Daly

Clarion Books is an imprint of Houghton Mifflin Harcourt Publishing Company.

www.hmhbooks.com

The text was set in Myriad Tilt.
The illustrations were executed in watercolor, pen, and digital media.

Library of Congress Cataloging-in-Publication Data
Daly, Niki.
Next stop—Zanzibar Road! / story and pictures by Niki Daly.
p. cm.
Summary: In Africa, Mama Jumbo puts on a jazzy dress, struggles to get her hat straight with no
mirror, then jumps in Mr. Motiki's taxi to go to the market, where she finds everything she needs and more.
ISBN 978-0-547-68852-7
[1. Markets—Fiction. 2. Elephants—Fiction. 3. Animals—Fiction. 4. Africa—Fiction.] I. Title.
PZ7.D1715Nex 2012
[E]—dc23   2011040114

Manufactured in Singapore
TWP 10 9 8 7 6 5 4 3 2 1
4500364001

Next Stop—
Zanzibar Road!

Story and Pictures by Niki Daly

CLARION BOOKS
Houghton Mifflin Harcourt
Boston • New York • 2012

CONTENTS

CHAPTER ONE
Hurry Hurry, Mama Jumbo!

The sun was up and Africa was as hot as a frying pan.

At Number 7-Up Zanzibar Road, Mama Jumbo put on her jazzy dress and her "Flippy-floppy, flappy-slippy, this-way-that-way pompom" hat.

Mr. Motiki's taxi was coming to take her to the market.

"Hurry and get ready, Mama Jumbo!" cried Little Chico.

3

"Is my hat on straight?"
asked Mama Jumbo.
"No, it's all this-way, that-way,"
said Little Chico.
Mama Jumbo fiddled with her hat.
"How's that?" she asked.
"A little more this way,"
said Little Chico.
"And hurry, Mama Jumbo!"

"Like so?" asked Mama Jumbo.
"No, no! A little more that way,"
said Little Chico. "Hurry hurry,
Mama Jumbo!"

"How's that?" asked Mama Jumbo.

"Back a bit," said Little Chico.

"Hurry, Mama Jumbo!"

She shoved it back

—too far.

It fell on the floor.

Oh, my! Mama Jumbo was
hot and flustered.
"I need a mirror to see
what I'm doing!" she cried,
shoving her hat on
her head any old how.

Toot! Toot!
Mr. Motiki was tooting his horn.
"Be good, Little Chico!"
called Mama Jumbo
as she ran to catch the taxi.

She almost ran into Bro Vusi, arriving just in time to
baby-sit Little Chico.
"Slow down, Mama Jumbo!" cried Bro Vusi.

CHAPTER TWO
Mama Jumbo Goes to Market

Mr. Motiki's taxi thumped and bumped down the dusty road.

It tooted, hopped, and skidded to a stop to pick up passengers along the way.

By the time Mama Jumbo piled out, her hat was sitting on the tip of her trunk. "A mirror would be such a help," sighed Mama Jumbo.

The market was busy, busy!
But that was fine, because Mama Jumbo
really LOVED a loud, busy market.

BRAIDS
CORN
ROWS
BEADS

SPICY
CORN

"Squeeze me once, squeeze me twice.

Just one more squeeze and I'll double the price!"

joked Louie-Louie.

Soon Mama Jumbo's shopping bag
was heavy with fruit and vegetables.
"What else do I need?" thought Mama Jumbo.
"Ah! A mirror!"

Kwela was selling mirrors
and other pretty things.

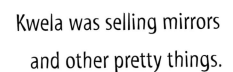

But when Mama Jumbo looked
in her purse, there was only enough
money for her taxi fare to get back
home . . . and a piece of half-chewed
Bum-Bum bubblegum.

Sadly, Mama Jumbo sat in the shade of a pawpaw tree.

Gadoomp! Two giant pawpaws landed in her lap.

"How lucky that they did not land on my

'Flippy-floppy, flappy-slippy,

this-way-that-way pompom' hat,"

thought Mama Jumbo.

Soon, Old Granny Baboon walked by, carrying
a basket of wooden beads.
"I'll give you my beads for your pawpaws," she said.
"Okay," said Mama Jumbo. "But I have only two pawpaws,
and you have lots and lots of beads."

"I know," said Old Granny Baboon.
"But my family is hungry, and we can't eat beads."
So Mama Jumbo and Old Granny Baboon swapped.

Next, Kwela walked by with all her pretty things.

When she saw Mama Jumbo's basket of beads, she said,

"I've been looking for beads like those for a long time."

"What will you give me for them?" asked Mama Jumbo.

"How about a mirror?" suggested Kwela.

Mama Jumbo wanted the mirror, but Kwela wanted those

beads *so-so* much! Mama Jumbo started to bargain.

"These are very special beads," she said.

So Kwela offered a mirror *and* a piece of African print cloth.

"Goody! That's a nice swap!" said Mama Jumbo,
waving her trunk from side to side.
What a lucky day at the market!

CHAPTER THREE
Mama Jumbo to the Rescue

Mr. Motiki's taxi went *toot-toot*ing and *bumpity-bump*ing
along the dusty road. All of a sudden there was
A GREAT BIG *THUMP-BUMP*—and the taxi stopped!
"All out!" cried Mr. Motiki.

Oh, my! A big thorn had punctured a tire. Mr. Motiki scratched his head and clicked his tongue. *"Tch-tch!* I don't have anything to fix the hole in my tire," he sighed.

"I do!" said Mama Jumbo. She dug in her purse for her yummy Bum-Bum bubblegum and gave it to Mr. Motiki.

"Hooray!" shouted the passengers as Mr. Motiki plugged the hole.

"Now you must put air in the tire,"
suggested Baba Jive.
But all Mr. Motiki could do was sigh,
"I don't have a pump
to put air in my flat tire."
"I do!" cried Mama Jumbo
with a little wave
of her trunk.

Mama Jumbo blew up the tire with one mighty puff.

"Hooray! Hooray!" shouted the passengers.

"Jump in!" cried Mr. Motiki, and they were off again.

On the way they sang a special song for Mama Jumbo:

"Zanzibar Road, here we come!

Hooray for Bum-Bum bubblegum!"

CHAPTER FOUR
Little Chico's New Shirt

"I'm home!" cried Mama Jumbo, arriving at Number 7-Up Zanzibar Road.

Mama Jumbo unpacked and made
a delicious fruit salad for their lunch.

"Mmmm," said Bro Vusi. "I'll baby-sit anytime!"

"I'm not a baby," said Little Chico.

"Of course you're not," said Mama Jumbo.

"And just you wait and see what I've brought home
for my big Little Chico."

21

Little Chico loved the fruity fabric.

So Mama Jumbo made a delicious tutti-frutti shirt for him.

What a shirt!

Little Chico skipped down Zanzibar Road,
showing his shirt to all the neighbors.

"Super-doops!" said Kwela.

"Sharp-sharp!" said Louie-Louie.

"Snazzy!"
said Bro Vusi.

"Jazzy!" said Juju.

But when Baba Jive

bent down and said, "Mmmm!

You look good enough to eat

in your new shirt!"

Little Chico ran all the

way home, crying

"Mama! Mama!"

When Mama Jumbo heard what Baba Jive had said, she laughed. "Oh, Little Chico, when someone says 'You look good enough to eat,' they don't mean they really want to eat you. What they mean is that you look adorable!" she explained.

Then Mama Jumbo held out her new mirror, so Little Chico could see exactly how adorable he looked in his new tutti-frutti shirt.

CHAPTER FIVE
You're Beautiful, Mama Jumbo

Before bedtime, Mama Jumbo looked into her new mirror.

Easy-peasy! On went her hat—just where a "Flippy-floppy, flappy-slippy, this-way-that-way pompom" hat should go.

But oh, dear! When she saw her big face looking back at her, she cried, "What big cheeks I have! And my nose looks like an enormous, fat sausage. How ugly I look in my new mirror!" "You're not ugly," said Little Chico. "You're the most beautiful mama in the whole of Africa!"

Then Little Chico sat on her head, and they both peered into Mama Jumbo's new mirror. "See?" said Little Chico. "Your cheeks are as soft as marshmallows. Your nose is nicely nosey . . . and *very* useful. And your eyes are big and shiny with love."

"Oh, Little Chico, thank you!" said Mama Jumbo.

"You really are too sweet for words."

"And good enough to eat?" asked Little Chico.

"You're the most adorable little chicken

in the whole wide world," Mama Jumbo said sleepily.

Then she lifted him off her head,

kissed him good night,

tucked him in,

and put out the light.

"Super-doops!

Sharp-sharp!

Snazzy! Jazzy!

And good enough to eat!"

whispered Little Chico,

gazing dreamily at the big African moon

peeping through the pawpaw tree

at Number 7-Up Zanzibar Road.

Bro Vusi

Louie-Louie

ZANZIBAR RD.

Kwela

Baba Jive